HORRID HENRY
WAKES THE
DEAD

Meet HORRID HENRY
the laugh-out-loud
worldwide sensation!

....

★ Over 15 million copies sold in 27
  countries and counting

★ #1 chapter book series in the UK

★ Francesca Simon is the only American
  author to ever win the Galaxy British
  Book Awards Children's Book of the
  year (past winners include J. K. Rowling,
  Philip Pullman, and Eoin Colfer).

"A loveable bad boy."
—People

"Horrid Henry is a fabulous antihero…**a modern comic classic**." —*Guardian*

"**Wonderfully appealing to girls and boys alike**, a precious rarity at this age." —Judith Woods, *Times*

"The best children's comic writer."
—Amanda Craig, *Times*

"**I love the Horrid Henry books by Francesca Simon**. They have lots of funny bits in. And Henry always gets into trouble!" —Mia, age 6

"My two boys love this book, and **I have actually had tears running down my face and had to stop reading because of laughing so hard**." —T. Franklin, parent

"**Fine fare for beginning readers**, this clever book should find a ready audience." —*Booklist*

"**The angle here is spot-on, and reluctant readers will especially find lots to love about this early chapter book series**. Treat young readers to a book talk or read-aloud and watch Henry go flying off the shelf." —*Bulletin of the Center for Children's Books*

"I have tried out the Horrid Henry books with groups of children as a parent, as a babysitter, and as a teacher. **Children love to either hear them read aloud or to read them themselves**." —Danielle Hall, teacher

"A flicker of recognition must pass through most teachers and parents when they read Horrid Henry. **There's a tiny bit of him in all of us.**" —Nancy Astee, *Child Education*

"**As a teacher...it's great to get a series of books my class loves.** They go mad for Horrid Henry." —teacher

"**Short, easy-to-read chapters will appeal to early readers, who will laugh at Henry's exaggerated antics and relate to his rambunctious personality.**" —*School Library Journal*

"An absolutely fantastic series and surely a winner with all children. Long live Francesca Simon and her brilliant books! More, more please!" —parent

"**Laugh-out-loud reading for both adults and children alike.**" —parent

"**Henry's over-the-top behavior, the characters' snappy dialogue, and Ross's hyperbolic line art will engage even the most reluctant readers—there's little reason to suspect the series won't conquer these shores as well.**" —*Publishers Weekly*

"will make you laugh out loud."
—Sunday Times

"**Kids will love reading the laugh-out-loud funny stories** about someone whose behavior is even worse than their own." —*School Library Journal*

"Humor is a proven enticement for reluctant readers, and **Francesca Simon's Horrid Henry series locates the funny bone with ease**." —*Newsday*

"**What is brilliant about the books is that Henry never does anything that is subversive**. [Francesca Simon] creates an aura of supreme naughtiness (of which children are in awe) but points out that he operates within a safe and secure world…**eminently readable** books."
—Emily Turner, *Angels and Urchins*

"**Kids who love funny books will love the Horrid Henry series** by Francesca Simon…Simon's hilariously dead-pan text is wonderfully complemented by Tony Ross's illustrations, which comically capture the consequences of Henry's horridness." —*Scripps Howard News Service*

"Accompanied by fantastic black-and-white drawings, the book is a joy to read. **Horrid Henry has an irresistible appeal to everyone—child and adult alike!** He is the child everyone is familiar with—irritating, annoying, but you still cannot help laughing when he gets into yet another scrape. Not quite a devil in disguise but you cannot help wondering at times! No wonder he is so popular!"
—Angela Youngman

Horrid Henry by Francesca Simon

....

Horrid Henry

Horrid Henry Tricks the Tooth Fairy

Horrid Henry and the Mega-Mean Time Machine

Horrid Henry's Stinkbomb

Horrid Henry and the Mummy's Curse

Horrid Henry and the Soccer Fiend

Horrid Henry's Underpants

Horrid Henry and the Scary Sitter

Horrid Henry's Christmas

Horrid Henry and the Abominable Snowman

Horrid Henry Rocks

Horrid Henry Wakes the Dead

Horrid Henry's Joke Book

HORRID HENRY
WAKES THE
DEAD

Francesca Simon
Illustrated by Tony Ross

visit us at www.abdopublishing.com

Reinforced library bound edition published in 2013 by Spotlight, a division of the ABDO Group, PO Box 398166, Minneapolis, MN 55439. Spotlight produces high-quality reinforced library bound editions for schools and libraries. Published by agreement with Sourcebooks, Inc.

Printed in the United States of America, North Mankato, Minnesota.

042012

092012

 This book contains at least 10% recycled materials.

Cataloging-in-Publication Data

Simon, Francesca.
  Horrid Henry wakes the dead / Francesca Simon ; illustrated by Tony Ross.
    p. cm.
  [1. Horrid Henry (Fictitious character)—Fiction. 2. Conduct of life—Fiction. 3. Behavior—Fiction. 4. Humorous stories] I. Ross, Tony, ill. II. Title.
  PZ7.S604Hrf 2009
  [Fic]—dc22

ISBN 978-1-59961-192-1 (reinforced library edition)

For Steven Butler,
the original Horrid Henry

CONTENTS

1

HORRID HENRY AND THE TV REMOTE

Horrid Henry pushed through the front door. Perfect Peter squeezed past him and ran inside.

"Hey!" screamed Horrid Henry, dashing after him. "Get back here, worm."

"Noooo!" squealed Perfect Peter, running as fast as his little legs would carry him.

Henry grabbed Peter's shirt, then hurtled past him into the living room. Yippee! He was going to get the comfy black chair first. Almost there, almost there, almost...and then

Horrid Henry skidded on a sock and slipped. Peter pounded past and dived onto the comfy black chair. Panting and gasping, he snatched the remote control. Click!

"All together now! Who's a silly Billy?" trilled the world's most annoying goat.

"Billy!" sang out Perfect Peter.

NOOOOOOOOOOOOOO!

It had happened again. Just as Henry was looking forward to resting his weary bones on the comfy black chair after another long, hard, terrible day at school and watching *Rapper Zapper* and *Knight Fight*, Peter had somehow managed to nab the chair first. It was so unfair.

The rule in Henry's house was that whoever was sitting in the comfy black chair decided what to watch on TV. And there was Peter, smiling and singing along with Silly Billy, the revolting singing goat who thought he was a clown.

Henry's parents were so mean and horrible, they only had one teeny tiny TV in the whole, entire house. It was so minuscule Henry practically had to watch it using a magnifying glass. And so old you practically had to kick it to turn it

on. Everyone else he knew had tons of
TVs. Rude Ralph had five ginormous
ones all to himself. At least, that's what
Ralph said.

All too often there were at least
two great shows on at the same time.
How was Henry supposed to choose
between *Mutant Max* and *Terminator
Gladiator*? If only he could watch two
TVs simultaneously, wouldn't life
be wonderful?

Even worse, Mom, Dad, and Peter
had their own smelly shows *they*
wanted to watch. And not great shows
like *Hog House* and *Gross Out*. Oh no.
Mom and Dad liked watching…news.
Documentaries. Opera. Perfect Peter
liked nature shows. And revolting baby
shows like *Daffy and her Dancing Daisies*.
Uggghh! How did he end up in this
family? When would his real parents,

the King and Queen, come and fetch him and take him to the palace where he could watch whatever he wanted all day?

When he grew up and became King Henry the Horrible, he'd have three TVs in every room, including the bathrooms.

But until that happy day, he was stuck at home slugging it out with Peter. He *could* spend the afternoon watching *Silly Billy*, *Cooking Cuties*, and *Sammy the Snail*. Or…

Horrid Henry pounced and snatched the remote. CLICK!

"…and the black knight lowers his visor…"

"Give it to me," shrieked Peter.

"No," said Henry.

"But I've got the chair," wailed Peter.

"So?" said Henry, waving the clicker at him. "If you want the remote you'll have to come and get it."

Peter hesitated. Henry dangled the remote just out of reach.

Perfect Peter slipped off the comfy black chair and grabbed for the remote. Horrid Henry ducked, swerved, and jumped onto the empty chair.

"…And the knights are advancing toward one another, lances poised…"

"MOOOOMMMM!" squealed Peter. "Henry snatched the remote!"

"Did not!"

"Did too."

"Did not, wibble pants."

"Don't call me wibble pants," cried Peter.

"Okay, stinky poo poo," said Henry.

"Don't call me stinky poo poo," shrieked Peter.

"Okay, wibble bibble," said Horrid Henry.

"MOOOOOMMM!" wailed Peter. "Henry's calling me names!"

"Henry! Stop being horrid," shouted Mom.

"I'm just trying to watch TV in peace!" screamed Henry. "Peter's annoying me."

"Henry's annoying *me*," whined Peter. "He pushed me off the chair."

"Liar," said Henry. "You fell off."

"MOOOMMMMMM!" screamed Peter.

Mom ran in, and grabbed the remote. Click! The screen went black.

"I've had it with you boys fighting over the TV," shouted Mom. "No TV for the rest of the day."

What?

Huh?

"But...but..." said Perfect Peter.

"But...but..." said Horrid Henry.

"No buts," said Mom.

"It's not fair!" wailed Henry and Peter.

Horrid Henry paced up and down his room, whacking his teddy, Mr. Kill, on the bedpost every time he walked past.

WHACK!

WHACK!

WHACK!

He had to find a way to make sure he watched the shows *he* wanted to watch. He just had to. He'd have to get up at the crack of dawn. There was no other way.

Unless…

Unless…

And then Horrid Henry had a brilliant, spectacular idea. What an idiot he'd been. All those months he'd missed his fantastic shows…Well, never ever again.

SNEAK.

   SNEAK.

      SNEAK.

It was the middle of the night. Horrid Henry crept down the stairs as quietly as he could and tiptoed into the living room, shutting the door behind him. There was the TV, grumbling in the corner. "Why is no

one watching me?" moaned the TV.
"C'mon, Henry."

But for once Henry didn't listen. He
had something much more important
to do.

He crept to the comfy black chair and
fumbled in the dark. Now, where was
the remote? Aha! There it was. As
usual, it had fallen between the seat
cushion and the armrest. Henry grabbed
it. Quick as a flash, he switched the TV
over to the channel for *Rapper Zapper*,
Talent Tigers, and *Hog House*. Then he
tiptoed to the toy cupboard and hid the

remote control deep inside a bucket of
multicolored blocks that no one had
played with for years.

Tee-hee, thought
Horrid Henry.

Why should he
have to get up to
grab the comfy black
chair hours before his
shows started when he
could sleep in, saunter

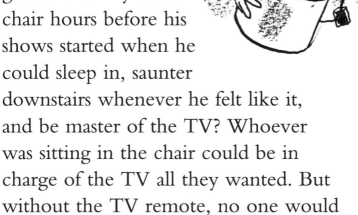

downstairs whenever he felt like it,
and be master of the TV? Whoever
was sitting in the chair could be in
charge of the TV all they wanted. But
without the TV remote, no one would
be watching anything.

Perfect Peter stretched out on the comfy
black chair. Hurrah. Served Henry right
for being so mean to him. Peter had

gotten downstairs first. Now he could watch what *he* wanted all morning.

Peter reached for the remote control. It wasn't on the armrest. It wasn't on the headrest. Had it slipped between the armrest and the cushion? No. He felt around the back. No. He looked under the chair. Nothing. He looked behind the chair. Where was it?

Horrid Henry strolled into the sitting room. Peter clutched tightly onto the

armrests in case Henry tried to push
him off.

"I got the comfy black chair first,"
said Peter.

"Okay," said Horrid Henry, sitting down
on the sofa. "So let's watch something."

Peter looked at Henry suspiciously.

"Where's the remote?" said Peter.

"I dunno," said Horrid Henry.
"Where did you put it?"

"I didn't put it anywhere," said Peter.

"You had it last," said Henry.

"No I didn't," said Peter.

"Did too," said Henry.

"Did not," said Peter.

Perfect Peter sat on the comfy black
chair. Horrid Henry sat on the sofa.

"Have you seen it anywhere?" said Peter.

"No," said Henry. "You'll just have
to look for it, won't you?"

Peter eyed Henry warily.

"I'm waiting," said Horrid Henry.

Perfect Peter didn't know what to do. If he got up from the chair to look for the remote, Henry would jump into it and there was no way Henry would decide to watch *Cooking Cuties*, even though today they were showing how to make your own granola.

On the other hand, there wasn't much point sitting in the chair if he didn't have the remote.

Henry sat.

Peter sat.

"You know, Peter, you can turn on the TV without the remote," said Henry casually.

Peter brightened. "You can?"

"Sure," said Henry. "You just press that big black button on the left."

Peter stared suspiciously at the button. Henry must think he was an idiot. He could see Henry's plan from miles away. The moment Peter left the comfy black chair Henry would jump on it.

"You press it," said Peter.

"Okay," said Henry agreeably. He sauntered to the TV and pressed the "on" button.

BOOM! CRASH! WALLOP!

"Des-troy! Des-troy!" bellowed Mutant Max.

"Go mutants!" shouted Horrid Henry, bouncing up and down.

Perfect Peter sat frozen in the chair.

"But I want to watch *Sing-Along with Susie!*" wailed Peter. "She's teaching a song about raindrops and roses."

"So find the remote," said Horrid Henry.

"I can't," said Peter.

"Tough," said Horrid Henry. "Pulverize! Destroy! Destroy!"

Tee-hee.

What a fantastic day, sighed Horrid Henry happily. He'd watched every single one of *his* best shows and Peter hadn't watched a single one of *his*. And now *Hog House* was on. Could life get any better?

Dad staggered into the living room. "Ahh, a little relaxation in front of the TV," sighed Dad. "Henry, turn off that horrible show. I want to watch the news."

"Shhh!" said Horrid Henry. How dare Dad interrupt him?

"Henry…" said Dad.

"I can't," said Horrid Henry. "No remote."

"What do you mean, no remote?" said Dad.

"It's gone," said Henry.

"What do you mean, gone?" said Mom.

"Henry lost it," said Peter.

"Did not," snapped Henry.

"Did too," said Peter.

"DID NOT!" bellowed Henry. "Now be quiet, I'm trying to watch."

Mom marched over to the TV and switched it off.

"The TV stays off until the remote is found," said Mom.

"But I didn't lose it!" wailed Peter.

"Neither did I," said Horrid Henry. This wasn't a lie, as he *hadn't* lost it.

Rats. Maybe it was time for the TV remote to make a miraculous return…

SNEAK.

   SNEAK.

      SNEAK.

Mom and Dad were in the kitchen. Perfect Peter was practicing his cello.

Horrid Henry crept to the toy cupboard and opened it.

The bucket of blocks was gone.

Huh?

Henry searched frantically in the cupboard, hurling out jigsaw puzzles, board games, and half-empty paint bottles. The blocks were definitely gone.

Yikes. Horrid Henry felt a chill down his spine. He was dead. He was doomed.

Unless Mom had moved the blocks somewhere. Of course. Phew. He wasn't dead yet.

Mom walked into the living room.

"Mom," said Henry casually, "I wanted to build a castle with those old blocks but when I went to get them from the cupboard they were gone."

Mom stared at him. "You haven't played with those blocks in years, Henry. I cleaned out of all the baby toys today and gave them to charity."

Charity? Charity? That meant the remote was gone for good. He would be in trouble. Big, big trouble. He was doomed…NOT!

Without the clicker, the TV would be useless. Mom and Dad would *have* to buy a new one. Yes! A bigger, better, fantastic one with twenty-five surround-sound speakers and a mega-whopper 10-foot super-sized screen!

"You know, Mom, we wouldn't have any arguments if we all had our *own* TVs," said Henry. Yes! In fact, if he had two in his bedroom, and a third one to spare in case one of them ever broke, he'd never argue about the TV again.

Mom sighed. "Just find the remote," she said. "It must be here somewhere."

"But our TV is so old," said Henry.

"It's fine," said Dad.

"It's horrible," said Henry.

"We'll see," said Mom.

New TV here I come, thought Horrid Henry happily.

Mom sat down on the sofa and opened her book.

Dad sat down on the sofa and opened his book.

Peter sat down on the sofa and opened his book.

"You know," said Mom, "it's lovely and peaceful without the TV."

"Yes," said Dad.

"No squabbling," said Mom.

"No screaming," said Dad.

"Tons of time to read good books," said Mom.

They smiled at each other.

"I think we should be a TV-free home from now on," said Dad.

"Me too," said Mom.

"That's a great idea," said Perfect Peter. "More time to do homework."

"What??" screamed Horrid Henry. He thought his heart would stop. No TV? No TV? "NOOOOOOOOOOOO! NOOOOOOOOOOO! NOOOOOOOOOOO!"

BANG! ZAP! KER-POW!

"Go mutants!" yelped Horrid Henry, bouncing up and down in the comfy black chair.

Mom and Dad had resisted buying a new TV for two long, hard, horrible weeks. Finally they'd given in. Of course they hadn't bought a big mega-whopper super-duper TV. Oh no. They'd bought the teeniest, tiniest TV they could.

Still. It was a *bit* bigger than the old one. And the remote could always go missing again...

2

HORRID HENRY'S SCHOOL ELECTION

Yack yack yack yack yack.

Horrid Henry's legs ached. His head ached. His bottom really ached. How much longer would he have to sit on this hard wooden floor and listen to Mrs. Oddbod twitter on about hanging up coats and no running in the corridors and walking down staircases on the right-hand side? Why were school assemblies so boring? If he were principal, assemblies would be about the best TV shows, competitions for gruesome grub recipes, and speed-eating contests.

Yack. Yack. Yack. Yack. Yack.
Zoom…Zoom…Squawk! Horrid
Henry's hawk swooped and scooped up
Mrs. Oddbod in his fearsome beak.

Chomp.
Chomp.
Ch—Wait a minute. What was she
saying?

"School elections will be held next
week," said Mrs. Oddbod. "For the
first time ever you'll be electing a
School Council President. Now I want
everyone to think of someone they

believe would make an outstanding president. Someone who will make important decisions that will affect everyone, someone worthy of this high office, someone who will represent this school…"

Horrid Henry snorted. School elections? Phooey! Who'd want to be School Council President? All that responsibility…all that power…all that glory…Wait. What was he thinking? Who *wouldn't* want to be?

Imagine, being president! He'd be king, emperor, Lord High Master of the Universe! He'd make Mrs. Oddbod walk the plank. He'd send Miss Battle-Axe to be a galley slave. He'd make playtime last for five hours. He'd ban all salad and vegetables from school lunches and just serve candy! And Fizzywizz drinks! And everyone would have to bow down to

him as they entered the school! And give
him chocolate every day.

President Henry. His Honor,
President Henry. It had a nice ring. So
did King Henry. Emperor Henry would
be even better though. He'd
change his title as soon as
he got the throne.

And all he had to do
was win the election.

Shout!

Shriek!

"Silence!"
screeched
Mrs. Oddbod. "Any more noise and
playtime will be canceled!"

Huumph, that was one thing that
would never happen when he was
School President. In fact, he'd make it
a rule that anyone who put their hand
up in class would get sent to him for

punishment. There'd only be shouting out in *his* school.

"Put up your hand if you wish to nominate someone," said Mrs. Oddbod.

Sour Susan's hand shot up. "I nominate Margaret," she said.

"I accept!" yelled Margaret, preening.

Horrid Henry choked. Margaret? Bossyboots Margaret, *president*? She'd be a disaster, a horrible, grumpy, grouchy, moody disaster. Henry would never hear the end of it. Her head would swell so much it would burst. She'd be swaggering all over the place, ordering everyone around, boasting, bossing, showing off…

Horrid Henry's hand shot up. "I nominate…me!" he shrieked.

"You?" said Mrs. Oddbod coldly.

"Me," said Horrid Henry.

"I second it," shouted Rude Ralph.

Henry beamed at Ralph. He'd make Ralph his grand vizier. Or maybe Lord High Executioner.

"Any more nominations?" said Mrs. Oddbod. She looked unhappy. "Come on, Bert, what would you do to improve the school?"

"I dunno," said Bert.

"Clare?" said Mrs. Oddbod.

"More fractions!" said Clare.

Horrid Henry caught Ralph's eye.

"Boo!" yelled Ralph. "Down with Clare!"

"Yeah, boo!" yelled Dizzy Dave.

"Boo!" hissed Horrid Henry.

"Last chance to nominate anyone else," said Mrs. Oddbod desperately.

Silence.

"All right," said Mrs. Oddbod, "you have two candidates for president. Posters can be displayed beginning tomorrow. Speeches the day after tomorrow. Good luck to both candidates."

Horrid Henry glared at Moody Margaret.

Moody Margaret glared at Horrid Henry.

I'll beat that grumpface frog if it's the last thing I do, thought Horrid Henry.

31

I'll beat that pongy pants pimple
if it's the last thing I do, thought
Moody Margaret.

"Vote Margaret! Margaret for president!"
trilled Sour Susan the next day, as
she and Margaret handed out leaflets
during playtime.

"Ha ha, Henry, I'm going to win, and
you're not!" chanted Margaret, sticking
out her tongue.

"Yeah Henry, Margaret's going to
win," said Sour Susan.

"Oh yeah?" said Henry. Wait till
she saw his fantastic
campaign posters with
the big picture of King
Henry the Horrible.

"Yeah."

"We'll see about that,"
said Horrid Henry.

He'd better start campaigning at once.
Now, whose votes could he count on?

Ralph's for sure. And, uh…um…
uhmmmm…Ralph.

Toby *might* vote for him but he'd
probably have to beg. Hmmm. Two
votes were not enough to win. He'd
have to get more support. Well,
no time like the present to remind
everyone what a great guy he was.

Zippy Zoe zipped past. Horrid Henry
smiled at her. Zoe stopped dead.

"Why are you smiling at me, Henry?"
said Zippy Zoe. She checked to see if
she'd come to school wearing
pajamas or if her jumper
had a big hole.

"Just because it's so nice
to see you," said Horrid
Henry. "Will you vote
for me for president?"

Zoe stared at him. "Margaret gave me a pencil with her name on it," said Zoe. "And a sticker. What will *you* give me?"

Give? Give? Horrid Henry liked getting. He did not like giving. So Margaret was bribing people, was she? Well, two could play at that game. He'd bring tons of candy into school tomorrow and hand them out to everyone who promised to vote for him. That would guarantee victory! And he'd make sure that everyone had to give *him* candy after he'd won.

Anxious Andrew walked by wearing a "Margaret for President' sticker.

"Oooh, Andrew, I wouldn't vote for her," said Henry. "Do you know what she's planning to do?" Henry whispered in Andrew's ear. Andrew gasped.

"No," said Andrew.

"Yes," said Henry. "And ban chips, too. You know what an old bossyboots Margaret is."

Henry handed him a leaflet.

Andrew looked uncertain.

"Vote for me and I'll make you Vice-Chairman of the Presidential Snacks Subcommittee."

"Oooh," said Andrew.

Henry promised the same job to Dizzy Dave, Jolly Josh, and Weepy William.

He promised Needy Neil his mom could sit with him in class. He promised Singing Soraya she could sing every day in assembly. He promised Greedy Graham there'd be ice cream every day for lunch.

The election is in the bag, thought Horrid Henry gleefully. He fingered the magic marker in his pocket. Tee-hee. Just wait till Margaret saw how he was planning to graffiti her poster! And wasn't it lucky that it was impossible to graffiti *his* name or change it to something rude. Shame, thought Horrid Henry, that Peter wasn't running for president. If you crossed out the *t* and the *r* you'd get "Vote for Pee."

VOTE FOR PETER

Horrid Henry strolled over to the wall where the campaign posters were displayed.

Huh?

What?

A terrible sight met his eyes. His "Vote for Henry' posters had been defaced. Instead of his crowned head, a horrible picture of a chicken's head had been glued on top of his body. And the *ry* of his name had been crossed out.

Beneath it was written:

"Cluck cluck yuck! Vote for a Hen? No way!"

What a dirty trick, thought Horrid Henry indignantly. How dare Margaret deface his posters! Just because he'd handed

out leaflets showing Margaret with a frog's face. Margaret *was* a frog-face. The school needed to know the truth about her.

Well, no more Mr. Nice Guy. This was war.

Moody Margaret entered the playground.

Be on Target
Vote Margaret

A terrible sight met her eyes. All her "Vote Margaret' posters had been defaced. Huge beards and mustaches had been drawn on every one. Beneath the picture, instead of "Be on target! Vote Margaret!" the words now read:

The next poster read:

How dare Henry graffiti over her posters! I'll get you Henry, thought Margaret. Just wait until tomorrow.

The next day was campaign speech day. Horrid Henry sat on the stage with Moody Margaret in front of the entire school. He was armed and ready. Margaret would be blasted from the race. As Margaret rose to speak, Henry made a horrible, gagging face.

"We face a great danger," said Moody Margaret. "Do you want a leader like me? Or a loser like Henry? Do you want someone who will make you proud of this school? Or someone like Henry who will make you ashamed? *I* will be the best president ever. I'm already captain of the soccer team. I know how to tell people what to do. This school will be heaven with me in charge. Remember, a vote for me will brighten every school day."

"Go Margaret!" yelled Sour Susan as Margaret sat down.

Horrid Henry rose to speak.

"When I'm president," said Horrid Henry, "I promise a Goo-Shooter Day! I promise a Gross-Out Day! With my best friend Marvin the Maniac presenting the prize. School will start at lunchtime and end after playtime. Gobble and Go will run the school cafeteria. I promise no homework! I promise skateboarding in the hall! I promise ice cream! And candy!

"If you vote for Margaret, you'll get a dictator. And how do I know this? Because I have discovered her top-secret plans!" Horrid Henry pulled out a piece of paper covered in writing and showed it to the hall. "Just listen to what she wrote:

Margaret's Top Secret
Plans for when I am President

The school day is too short. School
will end at 6:00 when I'm in charge

I look at my school lunch and I think,
"Why is there a dessert on my plate when
there should be more vegetables?"
All sweets and desserts will be banned

"I never wrote that!" screeched
Margaret.

"She would say that, wouldn't she?"
said Henry smoothly. "But the voters
need to know the truth."

"He's lying!" shouted Margaret.

"Don't be fooled, everyone! Margaret
will ban candy! Margaret will ban chips!

Margaret will make you do lots more homework. Margaret wants to have school seven days a week.

> There isn't enough homework at this School. Five hours of homework every night
>
> Get rid of school holidays. Who needs them?
>
> Ban chips!
>
> Ban football!
>
> Ban playtime!

"So vote Henry if you want to stop this evil fiend! Vote Henry for tons of candy! Vote Henry for tons of fun! Vote Henry for president!"

"Henry! Henry! Henry!" shouted Ralph, as Henry sat down to rapturous applause.

He'd done it! He'd won! And by a landslide. Yes!! He was President Lord High Master of the Universe! Just wait till he started bossing everyone around! Margaret had been defeated—at last!

Mrs. Oddbod glared at Henry as they sat in her office after the results had been announced. She looked gray. "As president, you will call the school council meeting to order. You will organize the bathroom tidy rotation. You will lead the litter collection every playtime."

Horrid Henry's knees felt weak.

Bathroom…tidy…rotation? Litter? What?? *That* was his job? That's why he'd schemed and bribed and fought and campaigned and given away all that candy?

Where was his throne? His title? His power?

NOOO!

"I resign!" said Horrid Henry.

3

HORRID HENRY'S BAD PRESENT

Ding dong.

"I'll get it!" shrieked Horrid Henry. He jumped off the sofa, pushed past Peter, ran to the door, and flung it open.

"Hi, Grandma," said Horrid Henry. He looked at her hopefully. Yes! She was holding a huge carrier bag. Something lumpy and bumpy bulged inside. But not just any old something, like knitting or a spare sweater. Something big. Something ginormous. That meant...that meant...yippee!

Horrid Henry loved it when Grandma
visited, because she often brought
him a present. Mom and Dad gave
really boring presents, like socks and
dictionaries and games like Virtual
Classroom and Name that Vegetable.

Grandma gave really great presents,
like fire engines with wailing sirens,
shrieking zombies with flashing lights,
and once, even the Snappy Zappy
Critters that Mom and Dad had said
he couldn't have even if he begged for
a million years.

"Where's my present?" said Horrid Henry, lunging for Grandma's bag. "Gimme my present!"

"Don't be horrid, Henry," said Mom, grabbing him and holding him back.

"I'm not being horrid, I just want my present," said Henry, scowling. Why should he wait a second longer when it was obvious Grandma had some fantastic gift for him?

"Hi, Grandma," said Peter. "You know you don't need to bring *me* a present when you come to visit. You're the present."

Horrid Henry's foot longed to kick Peter into the next room.

"Wait till *after* you get your present," hissed his head.

"Good thinking," said his foot.

"Thank you, Peter," said Grandma. "Now, have you been good boys?"

"I've been perfect," said Peter. "But Henry's been horrid."

"Have not," said Henry.

"Have too," said Peter. "Henry took all my crayons and melted them on the radiator."

"That was an accident," said Henry. "How was I supposed to know they would melt? And next time get out of the hammock when you're told."

"But it was my turn," said Peter.

"Was not."

"Was too, you wormy worm toad—"

"Right," said Grandma. She reached into the bag and pulled out two gigantic dinosaurs. One Tyrannosaurus Rex was purple, the other was green.

"RAAAAAAAA," roared one dinosaur, rearing and bucking and stretching out his bloodred claws.

"FEED ME!" bellowed the other, shaking his head and gnashing his teeth.

Horrid Henry's heart stopped. His jaw dropped. His mouth opened to speak, but no sound came out.

Two Tyrannosaur Dinosaur Roars! Only the greatest toy ever in the history of the universe! Everyone wanted one. How had Grandma found them? They'd been sold out for weeks. Moody Margaret would die of jealousy when she saw Henry's T-Rex and heard it roaring and bellowing and stomping around the yard.

"Wow," said Horrid Henry.

"Wow," said Perfect Peter.

Grandma smiled. "Who wants the purple one, and who wants the green one?"

That was a thought. Which one should he choose? Which T-Rex was the best?

Horrid Henry looked at the purple dinosaur.

Hmmm, thought Henry, I do love the color purple.

Perfect Peter looked at the purple dinosaur.

Hmmm, thought Peter, those claws
are a bit scary.

Horrid Henry looked at the green
dinosaur.

Oooh, thought Henry. I like those
red eyes.

Perfect Peter looked at the green
dinosaur.

Oooh, thought Peter, those eyes are
awfully red.

Horrid Henry sneaked a peek at Peter
to see which dinosaur *he* wanted.

Perfect Peter sneaked a peek at Henry
to see which dinosaur *he* wanted.

Then they pounced.

"I want the purple one," said Henry, snatching it out of Grandma's hand. "Purple rules."

"*I* want the purple one," said Peter.

"I said it first," said Henry. He clutched the Tyrannosaurus tightly. How could he have hesitated for a moment? What was he thinking? The purple one was best. The green one was horrible. Who ever heard of a green T-Rex anyway?

Perfect Peter didn't know what to say. Henry *had* said it first. But the purple Tyrannosaurus was so obviously better than the green. Its teeth were pointier. Its scales were scalier. Its big clumpy feet were so much clumpier.

"I *thought* it first," whimpered Peter.

Henry snorted. "I thought it first, *and* I said it first. The purple one's mine," he said. Just wait until he showed it to the Purple Hand Gang. What a guard it would make.

Perfect Peter looked at the purple dinosaur.

Perfect Peter looked at the green dinosaur.

Couldn't he be perfect and accept the green one? The one Henry didn't want?

"But I'm obviously the best," hissed the purple T-Rex. "Who'd want the boring old green one? Bleccchhhh."

"It's true, I'm not as good as the purple one," sobbed the green dinosaur.

"The purple is for big boys, the green is for babies."

"I want the purple one!" wailed Peter. He started to cry.

"But they're exactly the same," said Mom. "They're just different colors."

"I want the purple one!" screamed Henry and Peter.

"Oh dear," said Grandma.

"Henry, you're the oldest, let Peter have the purple one," said Dad.

WHAT?

"NO!" said Horrid Henry. "It's mine." He clutched it tightly.

"He's only little," said Mom.

"So?" said Horrid Henry. "It's not fair. I want the purple one!"

"Give it to him, Henry," said Dad.

"NOOOOOOO!" screamed Henry. "NOOOOOO!"

"I'm counting, Henry," said Mom.

"No TV tonight…no TV tomorrow…
no TV…"

"NOOOO!" screamed Horrid Henry.
Then he hurled the purple dinosaur
at Peter.

Henry could hardly believe what had just
happened. Just because he was the oldest,
he had to take the bad present? It was
totally and utterly and completely unfair.

"I want the purple one!"

"You know that 'I want doesn't get,'"
said Peter. "Isn't that right, Mom?"

"It certainly is," said Mom.

Horrid Henry pounced. He was a ginormous crocodile chomping on a very chewy child.

"AAAIIIEEEEE!" screamed Peter. "Henry bit me."

"Don't be horrid, Henry!" shouted Mom. "Poor Peter."

"Serves him right!" shrieked Horrid Henry. "You're the meanest parents in the world and I hate you."

"Go to your room!" shouted Dad.

"No allowance for a week!" shouted Mom.

"Fine!" screamed Horrid Henry.
Horrid Henry sat in his bedroom.
He glared at the snot-green dinosaur
scowling at him from where he'd
thrown it on the floor and stomped on
it. He hated the color green. He loved

the color purple. The leader of the
Purple Hand Gang deserved the purple
Dinosaur Roar.

He'd make Peter swap dinosaurs if it
was the last thing he did. And if Peter
wouldn't swap, he'd be sorry he was
born. Henry would...Henry could...

And then suddenly Horrid Henry had a wonderful, wicked idea. Why had he never thought of this before?

Perfect Peter sat in his bedroom. He smiled at the purple dinosaur as it lurched, roaring around the room.

"RRRRAAAAAAAA! RAAAAAAAAA! FEED ME!" bellowed the dinosaur.

How lucky he was to have the purple dinosaur. Purple was much better than green. It was only fair that Peter got the purple dinosaur, and Henry got the yucky green one. After all, Peter was perfect and Henry was horrid. Peter deserved the purple one.

Suddenly Horrid Henry burst into his bedroom.

"Mom said to stay in your room," squealed Peter, shoving the dinosaur

under his desk and standing guard in
front of it. Henry would have to drag
him away kicking and screaming before
he got his hands on Peter's T-Rex.

"So?" said Henry.

"I'm telling on you," said Peter.

"Go ahead," said Henry. "I'm telling
on *you*, wibble pants."

Tell on him? Tell what?

"There's nothing to tell," said Perfect
Peter.

"Oh yes there is," said Henry. "I'm going to tell everyone what a mean, horrid, wormy toad you are, stealing the purple dinosaur when I said I wanted it first."

Perfect Peter gasped. Horrid? Him?

"I didn't steal it," said Peter. "And I'm not horrid."

"Are too."

"Am not. I'm perfect."

"No you're not. If you were *really* perfect, you wouldn't be so selfish," said Henry.

"I'm not selfish," whimpered Peter.

But *was* he being selfish keeping the purple dinosaur, when Henry wanted it so badly?

"Mom and Dad said I could have it," said Peter weakly.

"That's 'cause they knew you'd just start crying," said Henry. "Actually, they're disappointed in you. I heard them."

"What did they say?" gasped Peter.

"That you were a crybaby," said Henry.

"I'm not a crybaby," said Peter.

"Then why are you acting like one, crybaby?"

Could Henry be telling the truth? Mom and Dad...disappointed in him... thinking he was a baby? A selfish baby? A *horrid*, selfish baby?

Oh no, thought Peter. Could Henry be right? *Was* he being horrid?

"Go on, Peter," urged his angel. "Give Henry the purple one. After all, they're exactly the same, just different colors."

"Don't do it!" urged his devil. "Why should you always be perfect? Be horrid for once."

"Umm, umm," said Peter.

"You know you want to do the right thing," said Henry.

Peter did want to do the right thing.

"Okay, Henry," said Peter. "You can have the purple dinosaur. I'll have the green one."

YES!!!

Slowly Perfect Peter crawled under his desk and picked up the purple dinosaur.

"Good boy, Peter," said his angel.

"Idiot," said his devil.

Slowly Peter held out the dinosaur to Henry. Henry grabbed it...

Wait. Was he crazy? Why should he swap with Henry? Henry was only trying to trick him...

"Give it back!" yelled Peter.

"No!" said Henry.

Peter tugged on the dinosaur's legs.

Henry tugged on the dinosaur's head.

"Gimme!"

   "Gimme!"

      Tug

         Tug

            Yank

               Yank

                  Snaaaaap.

                     Riiiiiip.

Horrid Henry looked at the twisted purple dinosaur head in his hands. Perfect Peter looked at the broken purple dinosaur claw in his hands.

"I want the green dinosaur!" shrieked Henry and Peter.

65

4

HORRID HENRY WAKES THE DEAD

"No, no, no, no, no!" shouted Miss Battle-Axe. "Spitting is not a talent, Graham. Violet, you can't do the cancan as your talent. Ralph, burping to the beat is not a talent."

She turned to Bert. "What's your talent?"

"I dunno," said Beefy Bert.

"And what about you, Steven?" said Miss Battle-Axe grimly.

"Caveman," grunted Stone-Age Steven. "Ugg!"

Horrid Henry had had enough.

"Me next!" shrieked Horrid Henry.
"I've got a great talent! Me next!"

"Me!" shrieked Moody Margaret.

"Me!" shrieked Rude Ralph.

"No one who shouts out will
be performing *anything*," said Miss
Battle-Axe.

Next week was Horrid Henry's school
talent show. But this wasn't an ordinary
school talent show. Oh no. This year
was different. This year, the famous
TV presenter Sneering Simone was
choosing the winner.

But best and most fantastic of all,

the prize was a chance to appear on Simone's TV show, *Talent Tigers*. And from there…well, there was no end to the fame and fortune that awaited the winner.

Horrid Henry had to win. He just had to. A chance to be on TV! A chance for his genius to be recognized, at last.

The only problem was, he had so many talents it was impossible to pick just one. He could eat chips faster than Greedy Graham. He could burp to the theme tune of *Marvin the Maniac*. He could stick out his tongue almost as far as Moody Margaret.

But brilliant as these talents were, perhaps they weren't *quite* special enough to win. Hmmmm…

Wait, he had it.

He could perform his new rap, "I have

an ugly brother, ick ick ick/A smelly
toad brother, who makes me sick."
That would be sure to get him
on *Talent Tigers*.

"Margaret!" barked Miss Battle-Axe,
"what's your talent?"

"Susan and I are doing a rap," said
Moody Margaret.

What?

"*I'm* doing a rap," howled Henry. How dare Margaret steal his idea!

"Only one person can do a rap," said Miss Battle-Axe firmly.

"Unfair!" shrieked Horrid Henry.

"Be quiet, Henry," said Miss Battle-Axe.

Moody Margaret stuck out her tongue at Horrid Henry. "Nah nah ne nah nah."

Horrid Henry stuck out his tongue at Moody Margaret. Aaaarrgh! It was so unfair.

"I'm doing a hundred push-ups," said Aerobic Al.

"I'm playing the drums," said Jazzy Jim.

"I want to do a rap!" howled Horrid Henry. "Mine's much better than hers!"

"You have to do something else or not take part," said Miss Battle-Axe, consulting her list.

Not take part? Was Miss Battle-Axe
out of her mind? Had all those years
working on a chain gang done her in?

Miss Battle-Axe stood in front of
Henry, baring her fangs. Her pen
tapped impatiently on her notebook.

"Last chance, Henry. List closes in
ten seconds…"

What to do, what to do?

"I'll do magic," said Horrid Henry.

How hard could it be to do some magic? He wasn't a master of disguise and the fearless leader of the Purple Hand Gang for nothing. In fact, not only would he do magic, he would do the greatest magic trick the world had ever seen. No rabbits out of a hat. No flowers out of a cane. No sawing a girl in half—though if Margaret volunteered Henry would be very happy to oblige.

No! He, Henry, Il Stupendioso, the greatest magician ever, would… would…he would wake the dead.

Wow. That was much cooler than a rap.
He could see it now. He would chant his
magic spells and wave his magic wand,
until slowly, slowly, slowly, out of the
coffin the bony body would rise, sending
the audience screaming out of the hall!

Yes! thought Horrid Henry, *Talent
Tigers* here I come. All he needed was
an assistant.

Unfortunately, no one in his class
wanted to assist him.

"Are you crazy?" said Gorgeous
Gurinder.

"I've got a much better talent than *that*. No way," said Clever Clare.

"Wake the dead?" gasped Weepy William. "Nooooo."

Rats, thought Horrid Henry. For his spectacular trick to work, an assistant was essential. Henry hated working with other children, but sometimes it couldn't be helped. Was there anyone he knew who would do exactly as they were told? Someone who would obey his every order? Hmmm. Perhaps there was a certain someone who would even pay for the privilege of being in his show.

Perfect Peter was busy emptying the dishwasher without being asked.

"Peter," said Henry sweetly, "how much would you pay me if I let you be in my magic show?"

Perfect Peter couldn't believe his ears.

Henry was asking him to be in his show. Peter had always wanted to be in a show. And now Henry was actually asking him after he'd said no a million times. It was a dream come true. He'd pay anything.

"I've got $6.27 in my piggy bank," said Peter eagerly.

Horrid Henry pretended to think.

"Done!" said Horrid Henry. "You can start by painting the coffin black."

"Thank you, Henry," said Peter humbly, handing over the money.

Tee-hee, thought Horrid Henry, pocketing the loot.

Henry told Peter what he had to do. Peter's jaw dropped.

"And will my name be on the billboard so everyone will know I'm your assistant?" asked Peter.

"Of course," said Horrid Henry.

The great day arrived at last. Henry had practiced and practiced and practiced. His magic robes were ready. His magic spells were ready. His coffin was ready. His props were ready. Even his dead body was as ready as it would ever be. Victory was his!

Henry and Peter stood backstage and peeked through the curtain as the audience charged into the hall. The school was buzzing. Parents pushed and shoved to get the best seats. There was a stir as Sneering Simone swept in, taking her seat in the front row.

"Would you *please* move?" demanded

Margaret's mother, waving her camcorder. "I can't see my little Maggie Muffin."

"And I can't see Al with *your* big head in the way," snapped Aerobic Al's dad, shoving his camera in front of Moody Margaret's mom.

"Parents, behave!" shouted Mrs. Oddbod. "What an exciting show we have for you today! You will be amazed at all the talents in this school. First Clare will recite Pi, which as you all know is the ratio of the circumference of a circle to the diameter, to 31 significant figures!"

"3.14159 26535 89793 23846 26433 83279," said Clever Clare.

Sneering Simone made a few notes.

"Boring," shouted Horrid Henry. "Boring!"

"Shhh," hissed Miss Battle-Axe.

"Now, Gurinder, Linda, Fiona, and Zoe proudly present: the cushion dance!"

Gorgeous Gurinder, Lazy Linda, Fiery Fiona, and Zippy Zoe ran on stage and placed a cushion in each corner. Then they skipped to each pillow, pretended to sew it, then hopped around with a pillow each, singing:

"We're the stitching queens
  dressed in sateen,
  we're full of beans,
  see us preen,
  as we steal...the...scene!"

Sneering Simone looked surprised. Tee-hee, thought Horrid Henry gleefully. If everyone's talents were as awful as that, he was a shoe-in for *Talent Tigers*.

"Lovely," said Mrs. Oddbod. "Just lovely. And now we have William, who will play the flute."

Weepy William put his mouth to the flute and blew. There was no sound.

William stopped and stared at his flute. The mouth hole appeared to have vanished.

Everyone was looking at him. What could he do?

"Toot toot toot," trilled William, pretending to blow. "Toot toot toot—waaaaaah!" wailed William, bursting into tears and running off stage.

"Never mind," said Mrs. Oddbod, "anyone could put the mouthpiece on upside down. And now we have…" Mrs. Oddbod glanced at her paper, "a caveman Ugga Ugg dance."

Stone-Age Steven and Beefy Bert stomped on stage wearing leopard-skin costumes and carrying clubs.

"UGGG!" grunted Stone-Age Steven. "UGGG UGGG UGGG UGGG UGGG! Me caveman!"

STOMP CLUMPA CLUMP

STOMP CLUMPA CLUMP

stomped Stone-Age Steven.

STOMP CLUMPA CLUMP

STOMP CLUMPA CLUMP

stomped Beefy Bert.

"UGGA BUG UGGA BUG UGG UGG UGG," bellowed Steven, whacking the floor with his club.

"Bert!" hissed Miss Battle-Axe. "This isn't your talent! What are you doing on stage?"

"I dunno," said Beefy Bert.

"Boo! Boooooo!" jeered Horrid Henry from backstage as the cavemen thudded off.

Then Moody Margaret and Sour Susan performed their rap:

"Mar-garet, ooh ooh oooh
Mar-garet, it's all true
Mar-garet, best of the best
Pick Margaret, and dump the rest."

Rats, thought Horrid Henry, glaring.
My rap was so much better. What
a waste. And why was the audience
applauding?

"Booooo!" yelled Horrid Henry.
"Boooooo!"

"Another sound out of you and you
will not be performing," snapped Miss
Battle-Axe.

"And now Soraya will be singing
'You Broke My Heart in 39 Pieces,'
accompanied by her mother on the
piano," said Mrs. Oddbod hastily.

"Sing out, Soraya!" hissed her mother,
pounding the piano and singing along.

"I'm singing as loud as I can," yelled
Soraya.

BANG! BANG! BANG! BANG! BANG! BANG! went the piano.

Then Jolly Josh began to saw "Twinkle, Twinkle Little Star" on his double bass. Sneering Simone held her ears.

"We're next," said Horrid Henry, grabbing hold of his billboard and whipping off the cloth.

Perfect Peter stared at the billboard. It read:

Il Stupendioso, world's greatest magician played by Henry

Magic by Henry
Costumes by Henry
Props by Henry
Sound by Henry
written by Henry
Directed by Henry

"But Henry," said Peter, "where's my name?"

"Right here," said Horrid Henry, pointing.

On the back, in tiny letters, was written:

Assistant: Peter

"But no one will see that," said Peter.

Henry snorted.

"If I put your name on the *front* of the billboard, everyone would guess the trick," said Henry.

"No they wouldn't," said Peter.

Honestly, thought Horrid Henry, did any magician ever have such a dreadful helper?

"I'm the star," said Henry. "You're lucky you're even in my show. Now shut up and get in the coffin."

Perfect Peter was furious. That was just like Henry, to be so mean.

"Get in!" ordered Henry.

Peter put on his skeleton mask and climbed into the coffin. He was fuming.

Henry had said he'd put his name on the billboard, and then he'd written it on the back. No one would know he was the assistant. No one.

The lights dimmed. Spooky music began to play.

"Ooooooooohhhh," moaned the ghostly sounds as Horrid Henry, wearing his special long black robes studded with stars and a special magician's hat, dragged his coffin through the curtains onto the stage.

"I am Il Stupendioso, the great and powerful magician!" intoned Henry. "Now, Il Stupendioso will perform the greatest trick ever seen. Be prepared to marvel. Be prepared to be amazed. Be prepared not to believe your eyes. I, Il Stupendioso, will wake the dead!!"

"Ooohh," gasped the audience.

Horrid Henry swept back and forth across the stage, waving his wand and mumbling.

"First I will say the secret words of magic. Beware! Beware! Do not try this at home. Do not try this in a graveyard. Do not—" Henry's voice sank to a whisper—"do not try this unless you're prepared for the dead... to walk!" Horrid Henry ended his sentence with a blood-curdling scream. The audience gasped.

Horrid Henry stood above the coffin and chanted:

"Abracadabra,
flummery flax,

voodoo hoodoo
mumbo crax.
Rise and shine, corpse of mine!"

Then Horrid Henry whacked the
coffin once with his wand.

Slowly, Perfect Peter poked a
skeleton hand out of the coffin, then
withdrew it.

"Ohhhh," went
the audience.
Toddler Tom
began to wail.

Horrid Henry
repeated the spell.

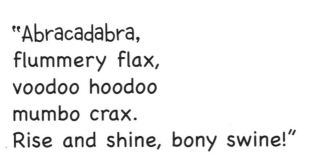

"Abracadabra,
flummery flax,
voodoo hoodoo
mumbo crax.
Rise and shine, bony swine!"

Then Horrid Henry whacked the coffin twice with his wand.

This time Perfect Peter slowly raised the plastic skull with a few tufts of blond hair glued to it, then lowered it back down.

Toddler Tom began to howl.

"And now, for the third and final time, I will say the magic spell, and before your eyes, the body will rise. Stand back…"

"Abracadabra,
flummery flax,
voodoo hoodoo
mumbo crax.
Rise and shine, here is the sign!"

And Horrid Henry whacked the coffin
three times with his wand.

The audience held its breath.
And held it.
And held it.
And held it.
"He's been dead a long time, maybe
his hearing isn't so good," said Horrid
Henry. "Rise and shine, here is the
sign," shouted Henry, whacking the
coffin furiously.
Again, nothing happened.

"Rise and shine, brother of mine,"
hissed Henry, kicking the coffin, "or
you'll be sorry you were born."

I'm on strike, thought Perfect Peter.
How dare Henry stick his name on
the back of the billboard. And after all
Peter's hard work!

Horrid Henry looked at the audience.
The audience looked expectantly at
Horrid Henry.

What could he do? Open the coffin
and yank the body out? Yell, "Ta-da!"
and run off stage? Do his famous
elephant dance?

Horrid Henry took a deep breath.

"Now that's what I call *dead*," said
Horrid Henry.

"This was a difficult decision," said
Sneering Simone. Henry held his breath.
He'd kill Peter later. Peter had finally

risen from the coffin *after* Henry left
the stage, then instead of slinking off,
he'd actually said, "Hello everyone! I'm
alive!" and waved. Grrr. Well, Peter
wouldn't have to pretend to be a corpse
once Henry had finished with him.

"…a very difficult decision. But I've
decided that the winner is…" Please
not Margaret, please not Margaret,
prayed Henry. Sneering Simone
consulted her notes, "The winner is the
Il Stupendioso—"

"YES!!" screamed Horrid Henry,
leaping to his feet. He'd done it! Fame
at last! Henry Superstar was born! Yes,
yes, yes!

Sneering Simone glared. "As I was
saying, the Il Stupendioso corpse.
Great comic timing. Can someone tell
me his name?"

Horrid Henry stopped dancing.

Huh?

What?

The *corpse?*

"Is that me?" said Peter. "*I* won?"

"NOOOOOOOOO!" shrieked Horrid Henry.

The HORRID HENRY books
by Francesca Simon

Illustrated by Tony Ross
Each book contains four stories

HORRID HENRY

Henry is dragged to dancing class against his will; vies with Moody Margaret to make the yuckiest Glop; goes camping; and tries to be good like Perfect Peter—but not for long.

HORRID HENRY'S UNDERPANTS

Horrid Henry discovers a genius way to write thank-you letters; negotiates over vegetables; competes with Perfect Peter over which of them is sickest; and finds himself wearing the wrong underpants—with dreadful consequences.

HORRID HENRY AND THE ABOMINABLE SNOWMAN

Horrid Henry builds the biggest, meanest monster snowman ever; writes his will (but is more interested in what others should be leaving him); starts his own makeover business; and manages to thwart the Happy Nappy for a chance to meet his favorite author in the whole world.

HORRID HENRY
ROCKS

Horrid Henry invades Perfect Peter's room; hunts for cookies in Moody Margaret's Secret Club tent, with frightening results; writes his biography— and Moody Margaret's; and plots to see the best band in the world (while his family wants to see the worst).

About the Author

Photo: Francesco Guidicini

Francesca Simon spent her childhood on the beach in California and then went to Yale and Oxford Universities to study medieval history and literature. She now lives in London with her family. She has written over forty-five books and won the Children's Book of the Year in 2008 at the Galaxy British Book Awards for *Horrid Henry and the Abominable Snowman.*